© for the Spanish edition: 2018, Mosquito Books, Barcelona
www.mosquitobooksbarcelona.com
© for the illustrations: 2018, Mikel Casal
© for the English edition: 2019, Prestel Verlag, Munich · London · New York
A member of Verlagsgruppe Random House GmbH
Neumarkter Strasse 28 · 81673 Munich

Prestel Publishing Ltd.
14-17 Wells Street
London W1T 3PD

Prestel Publishing
900 Broadway, Suite 603
New York, NY 10003

Library of Congress Control Number: 2018949222
A CIP catalogue record for this book is available from the British Library.

Translated from German by Paul Kelly
Copyediting: John Son
Project management: Melanie Schöni
Production management: Astrid Wedemeyer
Cover design: Nadine Clemens
Typesetting: textum GmbH, Feldafing
Printing and binding: DZS Grafik d.o.o.
Paper: Tauro

Verlagsgruppe Random House FSC® N001967

Printed in Slovenia

ISBN 978-3-7913-7383-6
www.prestel.com

My Town's (Extra) Ordinary People

Mikel Casal

Prestel

Munich · London · New York

Hi!

My name is Theo and I live in a small town by the sea.

A town just like any other, full of ordinary people like you and me.

People we might not pay much attention to at first.

But if we took the time to notice them, we might see that they are anything but ordinary.

They all have something that makes them unique, special, and interesting.

Would you like to get to know some of these (extra) ordinary people?

Peter

I watch as Peter goes down to the river at sunrise.

Every morning he hurries to his old rowboat waiting for him at the pier.

Across his shoulder he carries yellow oars, bright as a seagull's beak.

If you ask him why he is always in a rush, he will tell you how he loves
to pull the oars through the water as the boat glides up the river.

How he loves the drops of water that cool his face.

How the peace and quiet in the middle of the river carry him back to
his memories of the Olympics, where he competed many years ago.

We all admire Peter because he is steady and strong.

Carla

Everyone in our town knows Carla.

I have never spoken to her, but I often see her in the park surrounded by the birds that live in the trees.

All the birds know her because she always brings them seeds.

The closer she gets to the park, the louder the birds flap and chirp, as if they are saying to each other, "Carla is on her way! Carla is coming! Here comes Carla! There she is!"

They trust that Carla won't hurt them.

They eat straight out of her hands.

I would love to try that some time!

Henry and Nickel

Henry is the grandpa of my friend, Felix.

Nickel is Henry's Labrador.

You can always find the two together, gazing out at the sea.

Henry is an old sailor. For many years he was the captain of a fishing boat and traveled to distant places. Canada to Norway, Norway to Ireland, Ireland to Iceland ...

He has survived shipwrecks and watched whales and dolphins circle his boat. He has seen icebergs and even the Northern Lights.

He is full of seafaring tales. Felix's favorite is the one about how Henry found Nickel on a fishing boat when he was just a puppy. Though Henry hasn't sailed in many years, Felix thinks he can still smell the sea in his grandpa's clothes.

Felix

You have already heard of him. Felix is my best friend and the best skater I know.

He is full of ideas and always up to something new. Maybe he is inspired by the many stories his grandpa tells him. There's never a dull moment when you're with Felix!

When he's finished his homework, he likes to skate alone at dusk. He looks forward to this moment every day. Some find this strange. But Felix does not mind what others think of him. He is much too busy skating through life.

I'm lucky to have a friend like Felix.

Kim

"Nobody can play the guitar like Adam Jones!" says Kim.

"Who is Adam?" I ask her.

"He's the best jazz guitarist of all time!"

Even though Kim looks like a punk rocker, she is crazy about jazz and Adam Jones, her favorite guitarist.

Kim moved to our town to study guitar at the conservatory.

She gives music lessons and even performs on the street or in cafés so she can pay her rent and tuition.

She works hard to make her dream of becoming a professional guitarist come true.

One day soon she will be as famous as Adam Jones.

Alexandra

I often go with my dad to visit Alexandra's pottery shop in town.

We love to watch her work. We stare as her hands mold different shapes out of spinning clay.

It's like watching a magician make something appear out of thin air.

With only her hands and a lump of clay, Alexandra shapes beautiful and useful objects that please our senses.

Dave

Dave is a giant!

You might think I'm exaggerating, but when I see Dave on a rainy day, I get the feeling that his head is floating high above the clouds—or at least the umbrellas.

Truth is, Dave is shy about his height. He does not like to be noticed.

When he bumps into smaller people he turns bright red and wishes the earth would swallow him up. Which is a bit difficult given his size.

Everyone in town loves gentle Dave. Children who tug at his pants find themselves lifted onto his shoulders.

"I'm taller than Dave!" they shout.

And Dave, the gentle giant, smiles.

Mike

Mike is one laidback dude. He is never in a hurry.
I often see him cruising on his bike down to the beach,
his surfboard under his arm.
At the beach he slides into the water and waits to
catch the perfect wave.
After a most tubular day of surfing, Mike hops back
onto his bike and rides away with a blissful smile on
his face.
Mike is one chill dude. Hang loose!

Sara

Sara owns a bookstore.

All day she wanders back and forth between piles of books.

Each book takes her to a different world.

On Mondays she is a detective fighting crime. On Tuesdays she explores mountains, atoms, and outer space. Wednesdays, she only speaks in rhymes. Thursdays, she goes back in time. She is in love on Fridays and the weekends are filled with epic adventures far in the future.

I love going to Sara's bookstore.

She always finds the right book for me.

I can't wait to see where I'll end up next!

Jalen

Jalen makes art with shapes. His mind is all geometry.

When he looks in the mirror, his nose is a triangle, his body is a column, and his hair is in spirals.

He arranges dots, lines, waves, angles, and curves to make beautiful works of art.

Jalen says he loves to travel around the world because the earth is a perfect blue sphere filled with every type of shape imaginable.

Abigail

Abigail is a bookworm.

No matter where she is, her nose is buried in a book.

Sometimes she is so carried away by the story she is reading that she doesn't see her train pull into the station.

If she notices her train leaving without her, she just smiles and goes on reading.

Deshaun and Lorca

When Deshaun walks Lorca to school, he doesn't
talk about the football game from the night before.
He doesn't talk about the weather either.
No, when Deshaun brings his son to school, he
recites poetry.
Long, epic poems about love and bravery.
Short, quick ones full of wonder.
Japanese haikus that leap with surprise.
He also likes to make up poems. One of his favorites
repeats his son's name all the way to school.
Lorca, Lorca, Lorca ...

Jack and Selena

Jack and Selena have adored each other for many years.

They also enjoy spending time with their four grandchildren.

After fixing up a delicious snack, they like to take their grand-

children for a walk in the park.

They like to bundle everyone up, even if it isn't that cold.

If one of the grandchildren becomes frustrated, or another

starts crying, or all four grandchildren bubble up with feelings,

Jack and Selena are sure to give them the attention they need.

Afterward, they will prepare more delicious snacks.

They can't help being sweet and patient.

Violet

Violet is ten years old and does not hug anyone.

Not her parent's friends, not her cousins or aunts and

uncles, not even her grandparents.

She does not give welcome hugs.

She does not give goodbye hugs.

And she won't even spare a hug for a bag of

her favorite sweets.

Violet does not hug anyone because she does

not like hugging. And that's a fact.

I respect that Violet does not like to hug.

But it does not mean she does not like you or

that she does not enjoy a bag of sweets!

Glenn

When I hear piano sounds coming from across the street,

I know the time is exactly 6:35 p.m.

That's when Glenn sits down every day to practice his music.

Calm melodies fill the air as the sun sets.

Ogden

Ogden is my neighbor. His apartment is on the top floor.
During the day, he works in a restaurant. He brings salads
and chicken from the kitchen to table number 2 and table
number 5, then returns to the kitchen.
"A large chocolate ice cream for table 8!"
"On its way!"
When night falls, he hurries up to his apartment to spend
the night watching as many stars and planets as he can
see from his small window of sky.
The next day, he is back at the restaurant.
He moves around the tables like the planets orbit the sun.
All the while he dreams about returning to his homemade
observatory.
He can't stop thinking about the stars and planets waiting
to greet him in the night sky.

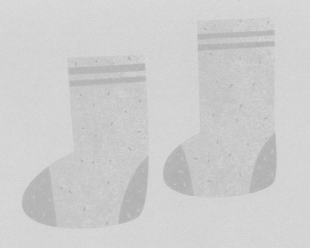

Emily

Emily loves stray cats.

Her doors are always open to any cat who wants to stop by.

There are cats on her balcony, in her living room, and even in her bedroom.

She loves cats, but Emily frowns when they scratch up her furniture. So she knits little white socks for the cats. Some have stripes, some have spots.

The cats feel safe with Emily and whoosh about on their socks across the floors of her apartment.

They are all happy and content in their warm and cozy paws.

Ayaan

Ayaan is very skilled with his hands.

He can fix, build, knock down, and put

anything back together again.

He is a free spirit ready to tackle any project

with his mind and his tools.

Ayaan has two nephews, Ismail and Rashid,

who he loves dearly.

He is always happy to play with them and likes

to invent games and activities for them.

One hot, summer afternoon, Ayaan filled the back of his pickup truck with water so that Ismail and Rashid could have their own pool to swim in.

Ayaan always comes up with the best ideas!

Zaza

If you could call anyone extraordinary, it would have to be Zaza.

He is elegant and extravagant.

He has a unique style. He never dresses like other people. He turns heads wherever he goes.

He looks amazing in his flower-print suit, pointy, star-studded shoes, and flowing, black cape.

He is always invited to parties.

Because when he has arrived, so has the party!

No matter how ordinary the people around you look, they are sure to have talents, hobbies, and stories that make them unique. There is something extraordinary in all of us—you just have to take a close look!